THE REAL UNREAL

RYAN WOLF

An imprint of Enslow Publishing
WEST 44 BOOKS™

Please visit our website, www.west44books.com.
For a free color catalog of all our high-quality books, call toll free 1-800-398-2504.

Cataloging-in-Publication Data

Names: Wolf, Ryan.
Title: The real unreal / Ryan Wolf.
Description: New York : West 44, 2024. | Series: West 44 YA verse
Identifiers: ISBN 9781978596689 (pbk.) | ISBN 9781978596672 (library bound) | ISBN 9781978596696 (ebook)
Subjects: LCSH: American poetry--21st century. | Poetry, Modern--21st century.| Poetry.
Classification: LCC PS584.W65 2024 | DDC 811.008'09282--dc23

First Edition

Published in 2024 by
Enslow Publishing LLC
2544 Clinton Street
Buffalo, New York 14224

Editor: Caitie McAneney
Designer: Tanya Dellaccio Keeney

Photo Credits: Cover VALUA VITALY/Shutterstock.com.

Printed in the United States of America

CPSIA compliance information: Batch #CS24W44: For further information contact Enslow Publishing LLC at 1-800-398-2504.

For Thomas Morrison
and Joshua Davidson,
seekers of the real.

Special thanks to
Caitie McAneney,
Ian and Kelly Richardson,
and my family.

Bright
  spirals
    screaming.

NEW WORLD ORDER SCUM
shouts across
the brick
in a sharp yellow.

FREEDOM WINS
waves beside it,
a proud blue.

WE WILL NOT OBEY
has a
grim green grin.

And
in the bloodiest
drips
of hot red,
it reads:

ALL
YOU
DEVILS
WILL BE
JUDGED

The graffiti
     is flung
everywhere.

Spat
on each side
of the building.
Sneering from
the limestone walls.

Bits of
broken glass
litter
the ground.
Sprinkled
     over
the sidewalk
like shiny
balls of hail.

What is left
of the windows
looks like
a thousand
tiny
teeth.

There are small gleams
of color
among the shards.

The stained glass
was over
a hundred years old.

But
what
does
it
matter?

Whoever did this
didn't care.

The vandals even
knocked
the nose
     off
one of the
gargoyles.

I don't know how
they reached
that high.

"NATE!"

For a moment
I imagine
the call comes
from the noseless gargoyle.

But when I turn,
it’s just Mrs. McMartin.

She is holding
    two brooms
    in one hand
        and a wad of
        trash bags
        in the other.

"We’re done
taking pictures
of the damage,"
she says.
"It’s time
for the cleanup.
But we’ve got this.
We’ll get through this
together."

She’s usually
standing tall
and smiling.

But now her
shoulders
are
slumped.

The wind breathes
    through the
        broken windows.

Through one opening
I can see
into a hall.

The vandals must
have climbed right in.

A cartoon cat
is splashed
on the wall inside.
Its eyes are
filled with
extra spray paint.
Deep red.

I know the image
instantly.

A cold chill
    claws at me.

It strums
and streams
down
my arms
        to the
        tips
        of
        my
        fingers.

What lies
below
the cat is
even worse.

A crumpled piece
of paper.

It yells:

WARNING

. . . CRIMES . . .

        . . . NOT SAFE . . .

Whoever came here
must have found them.

The flyers
in the street.

They believed
the message.
Took the warning
very
seriously.

"I'm so sorry,"
I say
to Mrs. McMartin.

I gaze above
the flyer.
Look away from
the filthy floor.

I am
staring
into
the scribbled circles
of the cat's
dead
eyes.

"I'm sorry,"
I repeat.
"I just didn't think . . .
I never thought that . . .
I didn't know . . ."

LOGGING ON

NORMIE

The summer
started off
pretty well.

I was working
as a dishwasher
at Smokey Sal's BBQ.
Dunking sticky dishes
into
soapy gray water.

I was signed up
for the summer arts program
at the Old Grand Lodge.
Ready to get
a few new pieces
done
for my portfolio.

Colleges
would see
how great
my work was.

They'd forget about
my grades.

My sister,
Emma,
was off in Europe,
studying something.
I didn't know
the details.

Mostly she was just
visiting
the big hitters.
London,
Paris,
Rome.

I was almost
happy for her.

My parents
worked crazy shifts.
So they weren't
home much.
But that was
alright.

As long as I kept
the place clean,
I could probably
get away
with anything.

I didn’t have
too much time
for trouble
though.

At least
not
at
the
start.

LATE

One night,
I was up late
playing
some street-racing game
online.

I was drinking
a bit of boxed wine
I had taken
from the basement.
My parents
would never
know.

It gave me
a little thrill,
I guess.
A taste of
the dark side.
Each sour drop
swished
under my
tongue.

My computer screen
seemed to brighten.
I felt its light
pulling me onward.
Lap after lap.
Track after track.
Circling,
     looping,
circling
     back.

The next morning,
I woke up
at 11:43 a.m.
I was supposed
to be at my shift
at Smokey Sal's
at 11.

My phone
was on *Silent*.
I had missed
my alarm.
Missed calls
and text messages
from work.

I didn't wash dishes
for Smokey Sal's
after that.

CANCELED

That Thursday,
I was supposed
to start my art program.
I'd gone every summer
since I was eight.
Now I was
almost 18.

The teachers said
they saw
"real promise"
in me.
I was building up
a folder filled with
drawings,
photos,
and printouts.
A portfolio.

My work was
the stuff of fantasy.
I liked to put
extra arms and legs
and eyes and ears
on creatures
and machines.

It felt like it
meant something.

I didn't know
what.

That Wednesday,
an email told me
classes were
canceled.
I guess the teacher
had the flu.
A few others
at the Old Grand Lodge
were sick also.
This was odd
for the summertime.

The local news
was calling it an
outbreak.
No one had died yet.
But people were already
taking this new virus
seriously.
It was a rare kind
that came from
farm animals.

During COVID-19,
there were still workshops
online.

But this time,
they were just
canceling everything.

I was happy
to do classes from
my computer.
I even sent an
email asking
about it.

They just said:

> **Dear Nate,**
>
> **We do not have the staff we need at this time.**
>
> **Have a good summer,**
>
> **Your Friends at the Lodge**

I wanted to
send back
a stream
of swear words.

But I didn't.

Instead,
I played the artist
alone
that night.

I tried to make
a few pictures
on my laptop.

I even shared them
on a message board
for fantasy art.

The pictures
were voted down.

Only one person
stopped to leave
a comment:

LOL

ZOOM

Emma
called the family
over Zoom.
She was
at a hostel
in Berlin.

She told us
about her tour
of the city.
Went on
and on
about walls
and gates.

She asked
about my art.
She asked
about my program.
She asked
about my job.

My parents
looked at
one another.

It had been
bad enough
breaking the news
to them.

Even if I
watered
the truth
down
a bit.

Emma had
so many
happy things
to tell us.

I could
feel her
beaming
through
the screen.

My parents
were beaming
beside me.

They were
so proud of
one
of their children.

RITUALS

I spent
the next day
applying for jobs.

And,
of course,
     cleaning
          every inch
               of the
               downstairs.

My mother
freaks out
if anything
is off.
When she
gets back
from the hospital,
she wants
"peace of mind."

This means
no mess,
of any kind.

Emma used to
tidy up
the place.
But now
I was filling in.

It seemed
pointless.

Wiping
crumb-free counters.

Mopping
already-shiny floors.

Scrubbing
an almost
spotless
toilet.

Pointless.

My father
could care less
about
cleaning
anything.
He never
bothers.

When he gets
back from the plant,
he just sits
at the kitchen table.
Pours himself
     bowl
     after bowl
          of bran flakes.

Skim milk only.

He watches
singing shows
on his phone.

His chewing
     is louder
          than
          the videos.

My mom
likes to put
medical dramas
on the TV.
She points out
all the parts
they get wrong.

She's been
a nurse since
before I was born.
So I guess she
knows better.

Mom always
falls
asleep
on the couch
in the middle
of a show.

She says
she doesn't snore.
But she does.

My parents
aren't usually awake
at the same time.
And when they are,
they are only
together
when we all call
Emma.

Or when
they are both
telling me
to get my life together.

My parents thought
it was weird that
the BBQ place
didn't need me
anymore.
But they didn't
ask too many
questions.

They never liked
the food
at Smokey Sal's
anyway.
Too much fat
and salt.

I really wanted to
"get my life together."

Whatever that meant.

So all day,
I sat in front of the computer
and applied
for job
after job.

Click,
     click,
          click.

Drive-throughs.
Bowling alleys.
Skating rinks.
Grocery stores.
All-night diners.
Once-trendy
clothing shops
in dying malls.

Did
anybody
want
me?

Or should
I just
stay home?

Should I
scrub the toilet
again?

Make another
pointless picture
for others to *LOL* at?

Text some "friend"
from school
who'd probably
never answer?

Stream a
spy thriller?
      Start a new
      video game?

Maybe a first-person shooter this
time.
Kill some zombies.

Fire away.
Click,
      click,
            click.

I didn't
know where
to begin.

There were
so many ways
to bury the hours.

So many
ways
to
take
up

empty

space.

NOPE

Turned out
most places
weren't hiring.

They were
worried about
the virus.

They were
worried about
possible
lockdowns.

They were
worried about
what they
didn't know.

They weren't
worried about me.

They didn't
owe
me
anything.

BOARD

I started going on more
message boards.
Not just ones for art.

I found
places where
people were
mad about
the job market.

Places where
people were mad
about the latest virus.

Places where
people were mad
about children's books
and superhero movies.

Places where
people were mad
about being born.

People were even
mad about
people being mad.

My username
was **The _ Seeker**.

What was I
seeking?
I don't know.

The name
felt right
to me.

I always
asked
too many
questions.

I liked to read
the comments
on the threads.
To watch
people claw
at each other.

Everyone was
angry about
something.

But that felt
right to me, too.

It made
sense
to rant.

Even if it
was just
about a pop song.
     Or an app game.
          Or a TV show.

People weren't okay.

Why should
they pretend
to be?

When no one
knew who you were,
you could say
whatever you
wanted.

You could be
more real
online
than you were
in the
so-called
real world.

You could
send
a stream of
swear words.

You could
scream.

/SECRETS/

There was
one site
whose name
I won't mention.

It had a
message board
called **/secrets/**.

I clicked around it
for a while.

I was **The _ Seeker**
after all.
Shouldn't I be
looking into
a few "secret" things?

There were threads
about all sorts
of strange stuff
I didn't believe in.
UFOs.
Bigfoot.
Shapeshifters.
Flat Earth.

Some topics
were more
grounded.
Drug running.
Cults.
Spies.

One thread
really caught
my eye
though:

FREE TRIPS 4 NORMIES

I figured I must be
one of those normies.

Someone
who lived a
boring,
normal
life
and was totally
clueless.

Whatever
the "trip" was,
it couldn't hurt
to learn
something new.

MEOW

At the top of the
FREE TRIPS 4 NORMIES
thread
was a picture
of a grinning cat.
Too many teeth
were tucked
into his
jagged
smile.

The cat's eyes
were glossy
and black.
Tiny swirls of stars
shimmered from
the centers of
those dark orbs.
Promising unknown galaxies.
Hidden worlds.

Beneath the cat
was a comment:

This is not a game.
Remember that.

This.
Is.
Not.
A.
Game.

Would you like to play?

Below the question,
a hyperlink glowed:

WHAT THEY DON'T WANT YOU TO KNOW

I held the arrowpoint
of my cursor
over the line.
It blared
      and blinked.

WHAT THEY DON'T WANT YOU TO KNOW

The cat's smile
seemed
to be
growing.

As if he wanted
to let me in
on all
his nasty
secrets.
Twisted
truths.

WHAT THEY DON'T WANT YOU TO KNOW

My finger felt electric.
It tingled as it
pressed
against the mouse.

I held it
for a moment.
Kept still.

Like the pause
before diving

    into a deep

    pool.

Then
I clicked.

HUNT

The link sent me
to another
website.

At the top
of the page,
it said:

COSMIC CAT CHALLENGE
Seek and find . . .

The cat was
underneath
the headline.

He puked out
a chain of circles.
Threw it
from his teeth
like a hairball.

Letters in a language
I didn't know
were written
over each circle.

I clicked
the top one.

The cat
slurped
up
the chain of circles.

Then spat out
an image
of a horned goat man
with wings.

                            up.
             pointed
One hand
The other
             pointed
                            down.

At the bottom
of the hand
pointing downward
was a search bar:

Type in Your Postal Code

I decided not
to enter mine in
yet.

I looked up
a code
for where
Emma was staying
in Berlin.

Pictures of
the Freemasons Grand Landlodge
in Germany
popped up.

Below them was a link:
READ MORE

Blaring
and blinking.

Click,
     click,
          click.

INFODUMP

The Freemasons,
or Masons for short,
had lodges
all over the world.

They started
late in the Middle Ages.
They were a
private club
that sometimes did
good things for
their communities.
But they also had
secret rituals
that many thought
were satanic.

A similar group
from Europe
was called the Illuminati.
They say
that club isn't around
anymore,
but some of
their members
became Freemasons.

There was a guy
in my grade
I went with once
to the movies.
He was a nerd
about politics.
He traveled to
Washington, D.C.,
most summers
for the Model United Nations.
He joked that
he was joining
the Illuminati.
He said
they ruled the world.

I didn't think much
of the idea.
There's too much
going on
for one group
to run everything.

But I could have been
wrong.

There was so much
on the site
I'd never learned.

I didn’t know
the Illuminati
were tied to the Freemasons.
And I didn’t know
that 14 U.S. presidents
were Freemasons.
Or that important
bankers in history
were Freemasons.

The history was pretty wild.

No one told me
there were so many
Masonic symbols
everywhere.
On the sides
of government buildings.
In Hollywood films.
On the cash
in our
pockets.

The pyramid
with the all-seeing eye
was on the
dollar bill.
That was
a trademark
the Freemasons used.

It was like
everyday people
were being
made fun of.

The winners
at the top
of the pyramid
were laughing
at us.

Even if the
Freemasons
didn't run *everything*,
it still
didn't
feel right.

Especially since
I hadn't heard
of them
until that day.

HOME

I typed in the
zip code
for our area.

Up popped
the Old Grand Lodge.

I guess
I never really
knew much about
the place's story.

I just thought of it
as a community center.

It did have
weird
stained glass.

The gargoyles
outside
used to scare me
when I was
younger.

I figured
it was probably
a church
in the past.

But what did
I know?

I rubbed
my eyes.
Pushed my
index fingers in
to shove back
a coming
headache.

The screen was getting to me.

I remembered
the art teachers
at the Lodge
pressing my
paint-soaked hands
onto sheets
of paper.

The squishy feel
of the many colors.
So many
years ago . . .

Too bad
the Lodge had
to let me down.

I'd have to do
more research
on them
later.

GENIUS

That night
we spoke
with Emma
on Zoom.

She was still
in Germany.
Munich now.
Another beautiful place
I'd probably
never visit.

I asked if
she knew that
Munich
was close to
the birthplace
of the Bavarian Illuminati.

She didn't.
My parents
raised their
eyebrows at me.
My dad had
a bran flake
stuck in his mustache.

I think
I sounded smarter
than usual.

It wasn’t
normal
for me to know
something
Emma didn’t.

She was studying
premed.
She would be
a doctor someday.
My mom stopped
at nursing.
My dad never went
to college.

They had
every reason
to think Emma was
some budding genius.

But I knew
something
she didn’t.

And if
even half
of what was posted
on **/secrets/**
was true,
what I discovered there
might be
bigger
than anything
Emma learned.

So this time,
when she went on
about castles
and creams,
I wasn't jealous.

I was
already
itching
to see
what else
the Cosmic Cat
had to say.

EDUCATION

That night
and the next morning,
I poured through
the Cosmic Cat website.

One of the circles
on the home page
led to leaked
government documents.

Another opened
a map of the world
that highlighted
places where people
went missing.

Another held
a list of wars
and who helped
pay for them.

There were charts
of famous families.
All the ways
they were connected.

There were
posts about
central banks.
I didn’t understand
most of them.

All the while,
at the top
of every page,
the cat
stared me down.

Daring me
to ask
more questions.
Find more
answers.

Learn all
the freaky facts
they never
taught
in school.

NAGGING

I forgot
to clean up
after my dad ate.

He left a ring
of skim milk
on the table.

My mom
screamed
when she saw it.
As if a spider
had landed on
her nose.

She'd had
an awful day
at work.
The hospital
was packed
because of
the virus outbreak.

She said the news outlets
were making
people panic.

I shouldn't
have missed
the stain.

But I'd spent
most of my day
on the computer.

Besides,
when I tried
to clean,
I couldn't focus.

I had a nagging sense
I still needed
to look into
the Old Grand Lodge.

I didn't want to.

It felt like
there was
a knife
at the throat
of my past.

I didn't want
to murder
my memories.

All those days
shaping clay
into little cups
for Mom and Dad.

Cutting up
magazines
to create collages.

Making my
first sketches
in pencil.

I drew
creatures
from the
deep
with endless eyes.

Always
searching.

Always
seeking.

What
should
I have
seen?

LURKER

So far,
on the message boards,
I was still
a "lurker."

I didn't write
any posts myself.

I didn't
comment on
the posts of others.

I didn't think
I had
anything
to add.

But then
I found a thread
that said:
OLD GRAND LODGE = CHURCH???

And I knew
it was time
for me
to speak.

OLD GRAND LODGE = CHURCH???

Big_King_White_Hat:
Anyone know the Old Grand Lodge in Upstate New York?
It used to be a Unitarian Church.
A church!
But then the devils took over in 1908. The Freemasons put up new windows. With eyeballed pyramids. Suns and moons hanging over pillars. Creepy as all get out.

The_Seeker:
But are any Masons still there?
It doesn't look like it on the Lodge's website.
Says they left in 1978.

Big_King_White_Hat:
Look closer at the groups that give.
The donor page shows Masons still paying them. Follow the $$$.

The_Seeker:
So? What does the Lodge do that's bad?

Big_King_White_Hat:
Well, they shut down right away with this new flu.
Mayor didn't even tell them to.
They're teaching people to be weak and afraid.

The_Seeker:
Maybe.
It sure sucks for kids this summer.
I live in the area.
Used to like the programs there.

Big_King_White_Hat:
I just looked more at their site.
They didn't shut everything down.
They kept the soup kitchen open.
And the food pantry.

The_Seeker:
Really?
Huh.
I guess those programs are important.
People need to eat.

Mockingbird:
dude, i know y they have to keep the kitchen open.
not what u think.
keep an open mind.
im sending u a chat.
in private.

PRIVATE CHAT

Mockingbird:
dude, the lodge puts stuff in the free meals they give out.

The _ Seeker:
For real? What kind of stuff?

Mockingbird:
to make people all cloudy in the head.
give them fluffy sheeple brains.

The _ Seeker:
Why?

Mockingbird:
so they dont rise up.
some people on the streets know things.
they need to dope em up.
make em look crazy.

The _ Seeker:
If that's true, shouldn't someone tell the police?

Mockingbird:
dude, they own the police.
McMartin, she runs the programs.
her brother is the police chief.

CLOSE

I looked it up.

Mary McMartin
was the Director of Programs
at the Lodge.

I used to see her
bouncy red hair
in the hallways.
She was always
high-energy.
Saying corny things
to cheer us up.

The chief of police
wasn't Mary McMartin's
brother.

But they were
cousins.

So Mockingbird
wasn't 100 percent
with his info.

But he was close enough.

PRIVATE CHAT

The _ Seeker:
I've taken classes at the Lodge.
They used to be cool there.
This year they were kinda cold.
But whatever.

Mockingbird:
ya.
not everyone who works there
knows much.
like how they move child slaves
thru the lodge.
but the whole devil vibe at the
place.
it has to rub off on everyone.
at some point.

The _ Seeker:
I never noticed anything that
weird.
Child slaves?!?!?

Mockingbird:
if i send u some videos . . .
will u watch?
i know it sounds crazy.
but this stuff is everywhere.
in every town.
u just have to know the signs.

HURT

I wish I never saw
what Mockingbird sent me.

People told stories
about things
I hope never happened.

I still don't know
what was true
and what wasn't.
But the stories
hurt me.

I won't reshare them.

Two things
felt clear enough.

It wasn't impossible
for the very rich
to do very bad things.

And it wasn't impossible
for bad things
to happen here.

PRIVATE CHAT

The_Seeker:
I'm speechless.

Mockingbird:
ya, its horrible.
the devil owns the world, man.

The _ Seeker:
I took classes at the Lodge.
I NEVER saw anything like those videos say.
Do you really think they are involved?

Mockingbird:
i know they are.
dude, they have satanic signs all over.
and i have very good intel
. . . someone on the inside.
he knows about the drugs in the food . . .
and about the kids . . .
and all the NWO stuff they push in lodge classes.

The _ Seeker:
NWO?

Mockingbird:
new world order.
where rich devil worshippers make the rules.
treat us like a bunch of cows to milk.
they can do anything they want.

CHOSEN

I rubbed my eyes.
Over and over.

Stretching the eyelids.
Pulling
them
down.

I remembered everything
the Cosmic Cat
taught me.
About bankers
and wars
and dark webs of power.
About the Freemasons
and the Illuminati.

It was all
     spinning
          together.

Melting
into one.

Mockingbird had
brought it all home.

Let my memories
be murdered.
I wanted

the truth.
The Lodge didn't care
about dropping my program.

The sticky paint
on my hands
was never
important.

I wasn't important.

The Lodge
had other plans.

They only cared
about what their masters
wanted.

If most of the building
was closed,
they could hide
their crimes.

They could go on
drugging the poor.

Did they ever
drug me
during snack time
or lunch?

Did things happen
I couldn't remember?

Mockingbird said
they could
get away
with
anything.

I shivered
at the idea.

Then a warmth
hummed
through my
body.

My thoughts
felt like
they came from
somewhere higher.

They were
beamed into
my skull.

I felt
the shock
of *knowing*.

I couldn't
prove
the story
about the Lodge.

But I *knew*
it was true
anyway.

Maybe
it was something
my body held.
A buried
memory.

A ragged ghost
hanging
in the back
of a forgotten closet
in my mind.

I shut off
my computer.
Looked out
my bedroom window
at the silent street.

It seemed
to hang on
a cloud.
Houses slipping
into mist.
Fences falling off
the edge of
the known world.
Unreal.

For some
reason,
the universe
had chosen me
to learn
a terrible truth.

I was
responsible
for it now.

DAZE

In the days
that came after,
I felt both
dazed
and more alive.

As I dusted off
shelves
until they squeaked,
I kept running
theories through
my head.

I glanced up
at the shelf
I was cleaning.
There was
a row of James Bond films
my dad owned.

Didn’t all those movies
talk about
evil masterminds
trying to take over
the planet?

Just seeing
those movies
felt like a sign.

I shouldn't
doubt myself.

I was on
the right track.

When I looked up
at the shelf again,
for a second
I thought
I saw a cat
perched at the top.

A toothy grin.

Mouth full
of fangs.

I didn't jump.
Just stared
as the image
faded.

There was
nothing there.

STEAM

Midnight.
I was in front
of a screen
with a cup of red wine.

The room
around me
was foggy.
Like the colors
were made
of steam.

A stack
of video games
by my bed
fell.
Almost
sent my heart
     hopping
from my chest.

I thought my mom
might have
opened the door.
Caught me
drinking.

She never
came in.

There was
no one but me.

I opened
one of my notebooks.

A cobra
with centipede legs
was drawn
on the first page.

No one
wanted to see that.

No one
wanted to see me.

But I could be
more than me.

I had to act.

I had to be
something.

I had to do
something
about the Lodge.

PRIVATE CHAT

The_Seeker:
How can I help??
I know we can't go to the police.

If the Lodge really is up to no good . . .
Shouldn't we spread the word?

Mockingbird:
definitely. people need to know.

The_Seeker:
I can print out flyers.
Tape them on lampposts.
What should I say?

Mockingbird:
just tell em the facts.
theres tunnels under the building.
so they can move drugs and slaves . . .
and bioweapons.

The_Seeker:
Whoa. Tunnels? Bioweapons?

Mockingbird:
ya, so they can poison whole cities.
it's part of the end game for the NWO.
they want to wipe out most of earth.
that way the elite can really have it all.

TUNNEL

In the morning,
my mouth
was tangy and dry.

My head felt fuzzy.
Too broken
to think.

This must be
how people
who had soup
from the Lodge felt.
Pulled toward a
tunnel within.
Where everything
was dark and warm.

Mockingbird
kept adding
to his story.

But he said he had
someone on the inside.

Someone who
knew things.
Someone who'd been
in the tunnels
underneath
the Lodge.

Of course,
I’d never seen any
tunnels there.
But I did remember
a locked door
in the art room.

Even with a hazy head
I could still
pluck
that memory out.

A white door.
There was
a poster pinned to it
that always
blew
my mind.

The poster had stairs
that went
in a square.

They were
forever going up
    and down
at the same time.

An unending loop.
Never getting
anywhere.

Maybe the poster
was a sign.
Another sick wink
from the "elite."

The NWO/
    Illuminati/
        Satanists/
            Whatever.

The names were getting
harder
to keep up with.
A trick on their part.
Keep everyone
too puzzled
to fight back.

I floated from
my bedroom
to the bathroom.

My face
fell
into
the bathroom sink.

I drank straight from
the faucet.
Spat most of the
water out.

It tasted too much
like wine.

I was still
an idiot.

But I'd learn.

FLYER

Coffee was
steaming
from an open travel mug
that said
GOOD MORNING,
SUNSHINE.

My head was
clearing up.

My hands rested
on my keyboard.

But I was
too scared
to start.

I had design skills.
Yet if I showed them off,
someone might know
it was me.

Posting flyers
about the Lodge
could be
deadly.

I'd need
to be very careful.

If the Lodge
was as dangerous
as I thought,
someone might kill me.

Actually
kill
me.

I tried to picture myself
cold and pale and dead.
Thrown in a dumpster
or a freshly dug hole.

The stakes were real.

But if the Lodge
had bioweapons . . .
The fate of
the world
might rest
on my stupid shoulders.

It was hard
to believe.

But it could be
the case.

I looked back
at my messages
with Mockingbird.
He seemed
serious.

Even though I was drinking,
I said I'd put up
flyers.

I should keep
my word.
Especially
if the Lodge
was *that much*
of a threat.

I'd need to
get the flyers up
at night.
Wear a face mask.
At least
with the virus around,
no one would
think twice.

I typed up
something quickly.

It sounded dumb
when I read it
back.

But maybe
it could make
people think.

They could
look things up
themselves.

If I was wrong,
they could
search around
and figure it out.

If there
was even
a tiny chance
Mockingbird
was right,
people needed
to be warned.

The words
I wrote
were blinking
into space.
Waiting for me
to set them
free.

I hooked
my laptop up
to my parents' printer.

Clicked **File**.

Then **Print**.

This
was
it.

WARNING

The Old Grand Lodge
at 33 N. Main St.
belongs to Freemasons!

An insider has said
there are tunnels
under the building.
They are used
for the worst **CRIMES**.
Children in the area
are **NOT SAFE.**

There may even be
TOXIC BIOWEAPONS.

Why haven't the police
looked into this?

What are they putting
in the meals
the Lodge gives out?

Where do the tunnels
beneath the Lodge go to?

Ask questions!
Find the TRUTH!

STAIRS

That night
Mom was working
a late shift.

Before Dad went to bed,
he must have watched
an hour of videos.

His eyes looked
bloodshot and
sunken
as he said good night.

"Any word on jobs?"
he asked me.

"No one's hiring,"
I said.

"Oh,"
he said,
rubbing his eyes
the way I do.
"Keep trying.
All you can do."

"But what if
everything's
rigged against us?"
I asked.

"It is,
in some ways,"
Dad shrugged.
"But we have
to keep going."

"Maybe
we're going
the wrong way,"
I said,
trying to keep
the meaning of
my words hazy.
"Maybe we worry about
the wrong things.
Maybe
there are big things
happening
in the background
that everyone
is missing.
Things we need
to worry about."

"Don't worry about
anything at all, Nate,"
said Dad
sleepily.
"Worry just
causes ulcers."

"What are ulcers?"
I asked.

"Holes in your
stomach,"
Dad said,
yawning.
"Your mom could
tell you about 'em."

I wanted
to say more.
To argue.
Warn him
about the darkness
all around us.

But Dad was already
halfway
up the stairs
by the end of
his sentence.

I imagined
the stairs
moving into
a square.
The steps
bent together
like in the
art room poster.
Dad walked
      and walked.
            Step after
                  step after
                        step after
                              step.

But he never
made it to
another
floor.

STAIN

Once I figured
my dad
must be asleep,
I found a
ratty old backpack.

I stuffed
the flyers
I'd printed
inside it.

I took an
N95 mask
from a box
my mom kept
near the door.

Even though
it was warm out,
I put a jacket on.
It made me feel
more hidden.

My pulse
was going wild
as I touched
the doorknob.
I could never
go back after this.

I turned to look
at my little home.
The shiny black
television.
The overdusted
shelves.

The couch
my mom snored on.
The kitchen table
where my dad
ate his cereal.

That's when
I noticed
a skim milk ring
on the table's surface.

I rushed through
the dark of
the living room.

Into the
still-lit kitchen.

I took out
a few sheets
of paper towel.
Slowly wiped away
the puddle.

Mom would
be happier
this way.

STREETS

It was
a 20-minute walk
to the Lodge.

Nothing too crazy.
But long enough for
someone
to see me.

I pulled
the hood
of my jacket
over my head.
Tightened the
string.

As I walked quickly,
the mask made
my breathing
feel more strained.
Like my lungs
were
shrinking.

Most of the houses
I passed
seemed dead.
Blank windows.
Perfect stillness.

I could see the flicker
and flash
of bright TV screens
from a few homes.

They glowed
in the shadows.
A smear
of blues and whites.

I was near
the end of my street.
Almost at the
stop sign.
Then a sudden scream
slashed
its way
through the night.

I jolted back.

Yellow light streamed
a few houses
from the turn.

Some kids,
probably in college,
had a garage door open.

They were playing
beer pong
in their underwear.

As I turned
their way,
I stayed on
the opposite side
of the street.
Hoping
they wouldn't
bother me.

Maybe one
of them called out.

I don't know.

I walked faster.
Breathed
even more
heavily
into the mask.
Until my lungs
felt full of flames.

I slowed down
when I reached
the next block.
Popped up
the top of my mask.
Sipped on
the air.

I was leaning
on a stop sign
when I heard

tires
squeal
to a stop.

An old Chevy
stalled in front of me.
A window
slid down.

"You okay, bro?"
the driver asked.

Snapping
the mask
back on my face,
I gave
a polite wave.

"I'm good,"
I said,
trying to
deepen
my voice.

Smoke from
the car's exhaust pipe
rose into
the night.

"Just checking, bro,"
the driver said.

The window slid
back up.

Tires screeched.

Red taillights
stared back at me
as the car drove off.

I quickly
crossed the road
and cut through
a park.

The sky was
cloudless.
The moon
almost full.
It disappeared
behind the trees
as I moved.

Wind ran along
the leaves of
giant oaks
and maples.
They swayed
over me,
guiding me on.

At first, I thought
I was alone.
Then I heard
the sharp shriek
of a swing.

Motion near
the rusty playground.

A lighter
clicked and
blazed,
cupped by
a hand.

Someone giggled.

I moved faster,
as far from
the swing sets
as I could.

The night
was after me.
It wanted to
fold itself over
all my plans.

But it
couldn't.

The moon
called me
onward.

My feet
moved
with the wind.

POST

I was on Main Street.
A block away
from the Lodge.

There was
a line of lampposts
running alongside
the street's shops.

I went toward
the nearest one.

It was in front of
Smokey Sal's BBQ.

I set my backpack down.

Unzipped it
with shaky hands.
Pulled out the papers.
Some spilled
     onto
     the sidewalk.

That's when
I realized
that I didn't have
any tape.
Nothing to put
the flyers up.

So much for not being
an idiot
anymore.

I looked at
the pole nearby.
It was covered
with other flyers
and stickers.

I tore down an ad
for some techno party.
Ripped the tape
from the edges
of that flyer
and used it
for mine.

It barely stuck
to the lamppost.
The tape was crinkled
and overused.

After some
struggle,
the flyer
stayed.
Somehow.

It looked
crooked.
But it was up.
Out in the world.

WARNING

It would shout
at anyone
who passed.

The words
would leap
from the page
into other minds.

They'd have
some effect.
Do *something*.

Headlights were
turning onto
the street.

I grabbed
my backpack.
Left the
rest of the flyers
blowing along
the sidewalk.
Fluttering over
 the curb.

Maybe
leaving them
would be enough.
Just to plant a seed.

If the flyers
blew away,
someone
would have to
pick them up.

They'd get
my warning.

I rushed off
into the shadows
of a side street.

It was too
risky
to stay.

I had done
something.

Something real.

There
behind my mask
in the
sprawling night streets,
I felt limitless.

MEDIA

The next day
I waited
for the news
to mention
something about
the flyers.

When my mom
came home,
she was
frazzled.
She wanted
to watch
one of her
medical dramas.

She made me
change
the station.

"Since when
do you watch
the news,
anyway?"
she asked.

She didn't even
mention
how clean
the place was.

I went upstairs.
Checked all of
the local news websites
to see if they had anything
about my flyers.

My heart pounded
as I searched.
I waited for my work
to flash across
the screen.

But of course,
there was
nothing
to see.

PRIVATE CHAT

The_Seeker:
I put up flyers. Not sure if
anyone spotted them.
I might check tomorrow.
The news didn't say anything.

Mockingbird:
why would they?!?
the lamestream media is part of
the NWO.
they only push their agenda.
the stories they want you to
hear.
almost nothing on there is true.

The _ Seeker:
Even on the local news?

Mockingbird:
if they are hooked up with the lodge and the police . . .
they def have plants in the news.
they will NEVER let the TRUTH out.

The _ Seeker:
How many people do you think are involved?
It's starting to sound like a crazy number.

Mockingbird:
probably is . . . not everyone knows everything.
a lot are suckers who get used.
they don't know they're being fooled.

SHUTDOWN

I went back
to the crosswalk
by Smokey Sal's
during the daytime.

I tried to go quickly,
so no one
at the restaurant
would notice me.

I didn't see
any trace
of the flyers
in the street.

There were
some to-go cups
from Smokey Sal's
crumpled
near a drain.
But no sign
of my work.

I went up
to the lamppost.

There was
a blank spot
where my flyer
had been.

It had either
fallen
or been
torn away.

Either way,
it was gone.

I could see
the black
of the lamppost.

The door
to Smokey Sal's
swung open.

I took off
back the way I came.

In the daylight,
I didn't feel
quite as limitless.

PRIVATE CHAT

The_Seeker:
They took the flyer down. I tried.

Mockingbird:
ya, i didn't see any out there.

The_Seeker:
You didn't see any?
You live here???

Mockingbird:
how do u think I know so much?

The _ Seeker:
Why didn't you put your own flyers up???

Mockingbird:
i guess i didnt think of it.
im usually a little harder core than that.

The _ Seeker:
Okay . . .

Mockingbird:
dude, changing topics, you know about CERN, right?
the supercollider in Switzerland
thats gonna kill everybody
tear a hole in the universe

SHIVA

I didn't know
about CERN.

Of course,
Mockingbird had links for that.

He had links
for everything.

CERN was a center
for nuclear studies.
They had a
supercollider
that tore apart atoms.
Tiny bits of matter.

Mockingbird showed me
a video
of some people in hoods.

They were at CERN.
Next to a statue
of Shiva.

Shiva was a Hindu god,
dancing in flames
on the back of a demon.
Building and destroying
endless worlds.

Spinning out
another loop
that wouldn’t stop.

Like the stairs
on the poster.

Like the chain
the Cosmic Cat
spat out
and drew back in
again.

Shiva had extra arms
stretching into
his ring of fire.
He reminded me
of my art.

The video was grainy.
Whoever held
the camera
couldn’t keep it
straight.

The hooded figures
were doing some kind of ritual.
Black magic maybe.

Toward the end,
it looked like
they stabbed
a woman in white.

I didn’t know
if the stabbing
was real or fake.

It reminded me
of another video
Mockingbird shared.
Where important people
who served in government
burned
a giant wooden owl.
Some said
they burned
a living human
inside it.

Mockingbird went on
to tell me how
someone who worked
at the Lodge
had a cousin
with a job at CERN.

I’m not sure
what the connection
meant.

But Mockingbird
told me
the final goal
of the New World Order
wasn’t killing us
with bioweapons.

They wanted

to rip

the universe

apart.

The supercollider
at CERN
could make
a black hole
so large
it would
swallow
our solar system.

Then it would grow.

A hungry wave
of darkness.
Chewing on
comets.
Eating at
every star.
Gobbling up
galaxies
like gumballs.

Every crumb
of life
and light
would vanish.
Gone.

There'd be
nothing
left.

PRIVATE CHAT

Mockingbird:
so after scaring u . . .
i meant to ask . . .
u down to meet?
like in the real world??

The_Seeker:
Uh . . . maybe?
Depends where and when.

Mockingbird:
at the lodge.
after midnight sometime.

The_Seeker:
That could work . . . but why
right there?

Mockingbird:
we can drop some more truth
bombs.
right in the big ole belly of the
beast.
tear them apart before they do
us in.

The_Seeker:
Truth bombs?

Mockingbird:
ya, man.
u got any spray cans???

PRACTICE

I found
an old spray can
in the basement.
I'd used it
for a summer project
at the Lodge.
We made
a model city
that year.

I laid out
sheets of cardboard
cut from broken boxes.
Shook the can.
Took aim.

Tssssss.

The paint
hissed.

I cracked open
an escape window.
Let the fumes
drift away.

Sunlight fell
on a wire rack
in a corner
of the basement.

I saw
the boxed wine
sitting there.
Promising to take
my edge off.

But I didn’t want
to sneak
any of that
anymore.

Alcohol
just kept people
     stupid
     and sick.

Tsssssss.

Circles.
     Spirals.
          Rings.

With each
push of my
thumb,
a blast of
black spray
     kissed
          the cardboard.

I began
to work on letters.

To shape them
in little bursts.

The first word
I wrote
came in
shaky streaks:

TRUTH

Sunlight
from the window
made
the black letters
shine.

I sprayed
a second
test word:

BOMB

It dropped
perfectly onto
the cardboard.

Like it was
ready to wake up
the sleepyheads
who didn't know
they were dreaming.

If they saw the real nightmare,
maybe it could be
stopped.

That's all I wanted.

Tssssss.

The paint shot
from the can.
Like a laugh spurting through
shut lips.

Two more
shimmering words
landed:

WAKE UP

FREAK

For once
my parents
were both there
at dinner.

We ate
together
at the kitchen table.
Gluten-free
noodles
in tomato sauce.
Sugar-free
lemonade.

Dad made
the meal.
Mom never touches
the stovetop.
Cooking is
a dirty job.

It reminds her
of the many messes
at work.
All that blood
and urine.

"So . . .
what have you
been up to?"
Mom asked,

more upbeat
than usual.
"You're keeping
the place
nice."

"You noticed?"
I asked, sharing a half-smile.

Suddenly,
I felt like I wanted
to tell my parents everything.

About the Lodge.
     The flyers.
          Mockingbird.

But I held back.

"I'm thankful
for you,"
she said.
"You help make this house
feel like home."

"We should
try to call
Emma tonight,"
Dad said,
sucking in a noodle.
"I hear she's now
in Switzerland."

The mention
of the country
tugged at me.
Begged me
to speak.

"Did you know
there's
a supercollider
in Switzerland
that smashes up
atoms?"
I blurted,
unable to hold back
any longer.
"One of
these days,
it's going to tear
a hole in the universe."

A fork clinked
against a bowl.

"Are you talking
about CERN?"
Mom asked
without a care.
"I don't think it
works that way."

"What do you know?"
I frowned,
caring very much.

"Have you even
looked into it?
Or do you just
listen to
the lamestream media?"

Dad chuckled.
"Lamestream media?
People are still
saying that?
That joke was bad
ten years ago."

"Not to mention we don't say
'lame.'
It isn't very nice
to people with disabilities,"
Mom said.
Her lips folded
into her own frown.

"Sorry,"
I said.
"I'm not meaning it
that way."

"I know,"
Mom said,
still serious.
"Just be careful
with the words
you use."

"But what
if I don't want
to be careful?"
I asked.
My cheeks glowed
red with heat.
"What if we can't
be real
because
we're all worried
about saying
the wrong thing?
What if terrible people
are trying
to destroy us
and we're worried
about
sounding nice?"

"What if?"
Dad said,
picking at his mustache.
"Is it wrong
to be nice?"

"Look, I'm talking
about us all
getting wiped out
because of CERN,"
I snapped.
"I don't want you to die.
Maybe I'm wrong to freak out.

But Emma is going to be
right near
the supercollider.
Isn’t that dangerous?
Do you really trust
the people
running these things?
Maybe they
want
to kill us.”

As soon as
I said that,
I realized
how weird
it sounded.

If that thing at CERN
killed everyone,
there would be no NWO.
No evil elite.
No world to rule
or control.

I could already
hear myself coming up
with a better story.
Ways to make
everything
fit together.

But maybe
they didn’t.
Maybe

the rituals
caught on camera
were a prank.

Yet there were
so many creepy videos.
So much proof
of so much darkness
in high places.

History was a tale
of the powerful
crushing the weak.

My parents
just didn't want
to see it.
They didn't want
to know.

If I loved them,
I had to protect them.

"Never mind,"
I said,
sitting back in my chair.
"I'll shut up now."

My dad
shrugged.
He scraped
the last of the pasta
from his bowl.

Then took out
his phone.

I slunk
even further
into my seat.

"Can you do
these dishes?"
Mom asked,
though
she wasn't done
with her own food.
"It'd be
a big help."

"Sure,"
I nodded.
"Of course
I will."

From the window
over the kitchen sink,
I saw the sky
turning pink.

Dusk would
arrive soon.

I was going
to meet
Mockingbird.

Tonight.

SHIFT

Mom and Dad
both had to work
night shifts.

The place
was all mine.

Once upon a time,
it'd be the perfect night
for wine.

But not now.

The spray paint
was in my backpack.
I'd printed
more flyers.
And brought tape.

I was going
to get things right
this time.

Even with a mask on,
I found myself
breathing easier.

It was cloudier
than the last night
I went out.

The clouds seemed
to cover my mind
with a thousand thoughts.

What if Mockingbird
was some type
of agent?

How did he
know some
“good guy” insider
after all?

I wondered what
he looked like.
How old was he?
Was he
even a “he”?

Would it be safe
going right up
to the Lodge?
They must have
cameras.

I might get killed.

I had to remind
myself
of this.

When I tried
to picture it

this time though,
it seemed so unreal.

I wasn't worried
anymore.
No ulcers
for me.

Besides,
if the worst
were true,
every single slug
and skunk
and squirrel
would die with me.

Tonight there was
no college party.
No too-friendly man
in a Chevy
rolling down
his window.

The park was
empty.
The swing sets
were still.
No wind
tickled the leaves.

This was
my night.

If I felt
limitless before,
I was truly
limitless now.

When I made it
to Main Street,
I didn't even bother
to glance at
Smokey Sal's.
Or the lamppost
where I'd stuck
my flyer.

No cars cared
to come my way
as I crept
closer to
the Lodge.

PIKE

I could see
the shimmer
of unlit stained glass.
The curved doors.
The hanging heads
of the gargoyles.
Guarding
their home.

At the end of
a parking lot,
someone was
leaning underneath
a window.
Its stained glass
held an open book.
Above its pages
was an ancient eye.
A drawing compass
fell like
a tear from it.

For a moment,
my pulse
picked up.

Could I trust
the figure beneath
the window?

"Mockingbird?"
I sent a loud whisper
across the lot.

The shape
shuffled.

"Hey, dude,"
a voice said.
It was scratchier
than expected.

As I came nearer,
I saw what looked like
a man in hunter's camo.
A black bandanna
covered
his mouth.

The figure
came toward me.

He wore a
a bulky backpack.
Bigger than mine.

His glasses glinted
under the streetlight.
As his face
floated closer,
I saw the lenses
were fogged.

The man
I knew as Mockingbird
stretched out a gloved hand.
I shook it.

He didn't seem
much older than me.

I couldn't tell for sure.

His handshake was very firm.
In a way that felt like
he was trying
too hard.

"The name's Pike,"
the man said.

For some reason,
I didn't think
that was true.
Were we
using code names?
Wasn't "Mockingbird"
enough of
a code name?

"You ready
to show
these suckers
we mean
business?"
Pike asked.

He never asked
for my
real name.

"I brought
some spray paint,"
I said.
"Figured
we'd drop
a few words
on the sidewalk.
It'd send
a message."

"The sidewalk?"
Pike sputtered.
"Dude,
we gotta tag
the building itself.
Make 'em
suffer."

"But . . .
the building
is beautiful,"
I said,
waving to
the stained glass.

"Seriously?
It's pure evil,"
Pike scoffed.
"They've got
tunnels full of slaves.

Stockpiles
of dirty bombs."

"Well, since we're here,
shouldn't we look
for the tunnels?"
I asked.
"I think there might be
one near
the art room . . ."

"Dude,
they'd kill us
the moment
we stepped inside,"
Pike said.

"Then can
they see
out here?"
I scanned
the parking lot.

"I guess,"
said Pike,
searching the dark
himself.
"We'll have to
be quick."

He slipped
his pack
from his shoulders.

It tumbled
onto the parking lot
blacktop.
Clinking
as it fell.

Pike unzipped
the top of the pack.
Inside were
three glass bottles
stuffed with rags.

In an instant,
my limitless
sense of
myself
fled.
Drained
from
my veins.

"Are those . . .
      Is that . . ."

I could hardly ask Pike
what I already
knew.

"Molotov cocktails,
my man,"
Pike nodded.
"Light 'em up.
Throw 'em.

And *boom*!"
I could almost
see Pike
smiling
through his bandana.

"If we can get
one of these
through a
window . . ."

He pointed to
the glass with
the compass teardrops.

"We just poke
the eye out of
that sucker,"
he said with a
light whistle.
"Then we set fire
to the Devil's den."

I shrank back.
Unsteady.

The glare
from the streetlights
      danced atop
      the bottles.

I could see
the labels.

They'd once held
Merlot.

Red wine.

"No way,"
I said,
trying to find
my voice.
"I didn't sign up
for this.
If there are people
in the tunnels . . ."

"Then they'll
have to let them out,"
Pike growled.

He picked up
one of the cocktails.
Held it by
the neck.

With his other hand,
he reached
into
his camo jacket.

He took out
a small silver gun.
Like something
from a Bond film.

Pike aimed
the pistol at me.

I froze.

The whole world
seemed to
freeze
with me.

FIRE

I was about to
cry out
when I noticed
the orange cap.
Winding around
the end of the gun.

Pike clicked
the trigger.
A blue flame
burst from
the pistol.

A lighter.
It was only
a lighter.

My relief
lasted less
than a second.

"Go ahead,
spray the sidewalk,"
Pike said.
"Write whatever
you want."

He moved
the lighter
close to the

wet rag
wilting
from the bottle.

I could smell
the gasoline.

"Time for this
baby to burn,"
Pike laughed.

He lowered
the lighter
more.

Let it lick
the edge
of the rag.

The flame
turned
from blue to yellow red.

It swept
    over the rag.
        Curling the
            fabric.

I couldn't
move.
Couldn't
think.
Only watch.

Pike raised
his arm.

He arched
his back.

Bent
his
elbow.

Aimed the
cocktail
toward
the sky.

PUSH

I sprang
to life
as the bottle
was about
to lift.

My head
went right
into
Pike's elbow.

He slid
     sideways.

The bottle

flew

upward.

Like a flaming baton
     twirling.

Then
it
dropped.

SPARKS

Upside-
down
fireworks.

Exploding
from
the pavement.

The cocktail
smashed
at Pike's feet.

Fire fingers
yanked at
his legs.

Dragged him
to the ground.

He rolled,
rolled,
rolled.

A burning barrel
of a body.

MEAT

The puddle
of flames
in the parking lot
shrank.
Sizzled and
smoked
on the blacktop.

I wanted
to run.

But instead
I went over
to Pike.

He was howling.

His right leg
was charred.

It smelled
like the barbecue
at Smokey Sal's.

Meat cooked
over a grill.

UNCLE

"What were you thinking . . .
why'd you . . .
how could you . . ."
the body groaned.

"You'll be okay.
I think . . .
We gotta get you
to a hospital,"
I said.

Leaning over
Pike's torn-up
pant leg,
I had to wince.

"No,
no,
no,"
he cried.

"Take me to
my uncle
instead."

SUPERCOLLIDER

It felt like
time was cut
to little pieces.

Each atom
of a moment
crashing into
the next.

Pike's arm
was draped
over me.

He limped
along
as I pulled him.

His foggy glasses
were cracked
and bent.

His clammy cheeks
were streaked
with tears.

TRUST

"My uncle . . ."
Pike kept mumbling.

The flames
in the parking lot
had died fully.

It didn't seem
like anyone
had seen us.

"Just point me
the right way,"
I said.

Pike's bandanna
had slipped.
His breath was
all over me.
It smelled like
weed and whiskey.

"Two blocks over.
That's it,"
he said.

I pulled him
in the direction
he wanted.

He was
still crying.

"You shouldn't have
pushed me like that,"
he said, biting his lip in pain.
"You should've
let me throw it."

"I wasn't out here
to burn down
a building,"
I told him.
"I mean,
what if we're wrong?"

Pike shook
his head.
Bit his lip
harder.

"You said
you had an insider,"
I continued.
"Who is it?"

"My Uncle Jamie,"
whispered Pike.
"He's online with us.
Big_King_White_Hat."

I knew the screen name.

From the first thread
about the Lodge.
"You cut into
my conversation
with that guy . . ."
I said,
helping Pike over
a sidewalk crack.
"You acted like
he didn't know much . . ."

"That's how we work,"
Pike said.
"It's a good way
to get the word
out there."

This sounded like
a setup.
This felt like
a trick.

"So your uncle
works at the Lodge?"
I asked,
trying to stay steady
as we moved.
"Who is he?
I might know him."

We turned
onto a side street.

"He doesn't
work there,"
Pike said
after a pause.

"How is he
an *insider*
if he doesn't work there?"
I asked.
"Did he break in?"

I was starting
to sweat.

"No,"
Pike said.
"It was just a manner
of speaking . . ."

"But . . . you said
he saw the tunnels,"
I half-yelled.
*"You said
he saw them."*

A dog barked.

A porch light
turned on.

I had to
quiet down.

"He *did* see the tunnels,"
Pike said
slowly.
"My Uncle Jamie . . .
he's psychic.
Dude can travel to
other places
in his mind.
He's been to all
the underground nooks
where they keep
weapons and slaves.
And technology they take
from alien visitors.
He's been to CERN . . ."
The dog barked
louder.

I heard the
sharp scraping of someone
taking out
their trash.

"Jamie knows things,"
Pike said.
"He says stuff
that comes true.
I didn't tell you
because a lot of people
don't believe it.
But he can travel
just by using his mind.
It's true."

"If Jamie can do that,
can he see us now
and come pick us up?"
I asked angrily.

"Just because
you're psychic,
it doesn't mean
you know everything,"
Pike sighed.

His body
was getting
heavier.

His white face
was getting
clammier.

"Why do you keep
questioning this?"
he asked with
a rattling breath.
"Why can't you
just believe?
I send link
after link
for everything I say.
I have
so much proof.
But it rocks your world
too much
to believe me.

I thought you
were with us, man.
Then you go and
set my leg on fire . . .
Just goes to show.
You can't trust
anyone."

PSYCHIC

Huge gray eyes.
Baggy and bloodshot.
The tan polo shirt he wore
was too small
for him.

He must
have only been
about 30 years old.

But this
was Pike's uncle.

Jamie.

Also known as
Big _ King _ White _ Hat.

The insider.

The psychic.

Whatever that
was supposed
to mean.

Jamie was at
the screen door
of the box-like house
Pike had led me to.
Hiding behind
the mesh.

To build trust,
I took off my mask.
In a low voice,
I told him everything
about the accident.

Partway through
my story,
he unlatched the door.
Pulled me
inside.

There were
several computer monitors
set up in what
must have been
a living room.
No couches though.
Only swivel chairs.

"I think Pike needs
to go to the hospital . . ."
I said.

"So after the hospital,
he can go to jail?"

Jamie hissed,
settling into one chair.
"You'd go to jail, too.
You're the reason
Billy got burned."

"Billy?"
I asked.
"Is that his
real name?

"Does it matter?"
Jamie screeched.
He tapped his fingers
on a desk.

Pike was about
to pass out.
His leg looked
chewed up.
Like the dog
barking outside
had gotten to him.

"You can just
throw him
into one of the chairs,"
said Jamie,
turning away.

I carefully
set Pike down
in a swivel chair.

The screensaver
on the computer
beside him
was a green spiral.
Tunneling on
and on.

Pike could barely sit up.
He slumped against
the monitor.

I held him in the chair
so he didn't
fall
to the floor.

Uncle Jamie
was still
looking away.

"Do you have
a blanket for him?"
I asked.

Uncle Jamie shook
as he rose
from his seat.

He went into
a darkened room
and came back with
a towel.

I wrapped it
around
Pike's leg.

I wasn't sure
this was right.

My mom would
probably say
I was sloppier
than the actors
in her medical dramas.

As I straightened
Pike out,
I tried to speak
to Jamie.

"So Pike said
you were an insider
at the Lodge.
He had a funny meaning
for that though . . .
It just meant
that you fly places
in your head."

"Sure,"
Jamie said,
annoyed.
"I can travel
on the astral plane."

I felt myself
starting to crack.
"I can't . . .
how am I . . .
I never wanted
anything like this.
I just wanted
to help everyone.
All I wanted
was some
truth . . ."

"What is truth?"
Jamie smirked.
"It's what the elites
want you
to think it is.
You have to
unhook yourself
from their ways.
The fact that
you don't believe
I could possibly
use my mind
to travel to other places
is a problem."

Pike moaned
and turned in his chair.
The towel
slid off his leg.

"No,"
I said,
"The *real* problem is
that Pike's, or Billy's, leg
is badly burned.
He needs
treatment."

"The leg will heal,"
said Jamie,
looking away again.
"It just needs
to be cauterized."

"Cauterized?
Do you even know
what that means?"
I said,
cracking
even more.
"That's when
you burn
an open cut
so it doesn't get
infected."

With my mother
being a nurse,
I at least
knew that.

"Then that's
what you
should do,"
said Jamie.
"Does Billy
have his lighter
on him?"

My jaw
dropped.

"You want to
burn
a *burn*?"

"No . . .
Not at all . . ."
Jamie stumbled
over his words.
"The leg should be frozen.
Help me put
his leg
in the freezer."

Before I could
question the idea,
Jamie grabbed
Pike from the chair.
He was much bigger
than him
but still wanted
my help.

Pike's sweat dripped
against my cheek
as we carried him
into the kitchen.

Jamie opened
the freezer
above his fridge.
We shoved Pike's leg
where he kept
trays of ice.

Pike roared
in pain.

An ice tray was
jammed into
part of his leg.

We pulled back.
Set Pike on
the floor.

Blood flowed
brightly
onto
the tiles.

Jamie grew as clammy
as Pike was.

His big eyes widened
even more.

Then his cheeks
ballooned.
Jamie tried
to turn.

But vomit
spurted out
the sides of his mouth.

The chunky acid
dripped
right
onto
Pike's leg.

If Pike
was roaring before,
the sound
he made next
was far worse.

Jamie ran to
the kitchen sink.

"Can't do blood . . ."
he said,
spitting out
the last bit of puke.
"I hate it.
Can't stand blood . . ."

I took some napkins
from the counter.

Tried to brush off
the clumps of vomit
from Pike's
bleeding leg.
Like I was
wiping away
a mess my father left.

Pike kept
howling at me.

Balling
his fists
like a toddler.

Kicking with
     his free leg.

One kick
landed square
     on my chin.

          Knocked me
          back
          against the wall.

My head hit
with a hard thud.

I was surprised
to see Jamie's hand
reaching
to help me up.

It was
still soaked
with puke.

I grasped
the slimy palm.

"Alright,
we'll do it,
kid . . ."
Jamie coughed.
"We'll drop Billy off
in front of
the hospital.
Make up
a story about
what happened.
Just no more blood.
     No more blood . . ."

UPRISING

Jamie's van
was covered
with stickers.
Flying saucers.
Chemtrails pouring
from a plane.
A tube full of green goo.
A slice of pizza.
The Shiva
from CERN.

So many stickers
had eyes.
It made the van
seem like
it could see
in all directions.

It could have been
straight out of
one of my drawings.

On the passenger door
was a sticker
I should've
expected.

The Cosmic Cat.
Grinning and
gazing.

Happy to see me
again.

We'd shoved
Pike into the back seat.
On top of a pile
of sandwich wrappers
and empty bags
from Smokey Sal's.

The towel was
wound tighter
around his leg now.
He was half asleep,
but moaned
that we'd forgotten
his backpack.

It was still
in the parking lot
at the Lodge.

When we swung
by there,
I hopped out.
Snatched the pack.

It was still open.
Unused cocktails
clinking.

The lot reeked
of gasoline.
I almost stepped on
broken glass.
But otherwise,
it was hard to tell
what had happened there.

I threw the backpack
beside the wrappers.
Jumped back in the van.

I sat in silence
as we peeled out
of the parking lot.

"You seem
like a nice kid,"
Jamie said,
finally breaking
the quiet.
"I'm sorry
this happened.
Billy shouldn't
have had
those Molotovs.
We weren't ready
for something like that."

I didn't say
anything.
I didn't want
to talk.

"Someday,
there'll be
a real uprising,"
Jamie continued.
"Everyone
will wake up.
Take the right pill.
See the world
for what it is.
There aren't
enough believers yet.
But there will be."

HOSPITAL

When Jamie pulled up
to the Emergency area,
he didn't offer
to help with Pike.

He didn't want
to be seen.

Pike was fully out now.
I dragged him from
the back seat.
Dropped him onto
the pavement.

Through the glass doors,
I saw a security guard
staring at us.

Jamie must have
seen him too.
Before I could
get back in
the van,
he floored it.

Jamie's head was
turned back
toward me
as he tore away.

He wasn't
paying attention
to what was
in front of him.

An ambulance
was pulling in
just as he was
pulling out.

The bumpers
banged
together.
They made
a snapping sound.

A crack
     and a pop.

Jamie's van
     was thrown
sideways.

It skidded into
     a parked truck.

Jamie spun
his wheels.

But the van
was stuck
     between
the truck and the ambulance.

After some
shouting and swearing,
     Jamie leapt
     out of the van.

He took off,
     racing into
          the night.

The security guard
was running
out of the building
by then.

I was still
crouched
on the pavement.

Holding onto
Pike.

"What happened?"
the guard screamed.
"What just . . ."

I wanted to
yell with him.

Or did I want
to laugh?

I settled
for staring
at the hospital doors.

Inside,
my mother had
stepped into sight.
She was in
scrubs,
holding some
loose papers.

Our eyes
locked.
Puzzle pieces
joining together.

I was done for.

LOGGING OFF

VIRUS

The rest of the summer
was all about
sorting out
what came before.

I was arrested
and booked.
So strange
and unreal.
Wearing handcuffs.
Sitting in the back
of a cop car.
Getting my
picture taken.
Rolling my
fingerprints.

My life was
a movie
or a TV show.
It wasn't mine.
It was someone
else's.

I told the officers
everything.

I didn't lie.

They searched
my phone
and later my computer.

They found
the spray paint
in my backpack.

The Molotov cocktails
were still in
Jamie's van.
I heard both he and Pike
were charged for them.
Along with
a few other things.

In the end,
I was only charged
with a misdemeanor.
Criminal trespassing.

That wasn't as bad
as it could have been.

I was only in trouble
for going on
the Lodge's property
at night.

For my sentence,
I was given
100 hours of community service.

Mary McMartin
from the Lodge
asked that I do
the service with them.

Part of me
was scared
this was
some NWO trap.
But I knew
it was meant to be
an act of grace.
A gentle sort
of justice.

Even though
the entire Lodge
was fully open
at this time,
they had me work
in the soup kitchen.

During lunch,
I'd eat the same meals
we fed to others.
I never felt dizzy
or passed out.

There were
no drugs.

Staff even let me
into the art room

at one point.
The same poster
I remembered
was on the white door
at the back of the room.

Mrs. McMartin
unlocked it
for me.

Inside,
there wasn't
the mouth of a tunnel.
Only shelves
filled with art supplies.
Canvases and brushes.
Bricks of modeling clay.

I was ashamed.
Though I partly wondered
if there was something
beyond the shelves . . .

"You have to be
careful with rumors,"
Mrs. McMartin said.
"They can spread
like a virus.
And make people
just as sick."

She told me
how most of

what I thought
about the Freemasons
came from rumors.

They were a men’s club
that gave to charity.
They had their own
rules and rituals.
But they weren’t
satanists.

The only connection
the Lodge had
to the Masons now
was a small donation
they received each year.
This was because
some Freemasons
were still proud of
the building and
its history.

They had no impact
on its programs.

At the end
of my 100 hours,
Mrs. McMartin asked
if I wanted to
stay on
as a paid intern.

I said yes.

So I had a job again.
Finally.

Feeding the hungry.
Scooping steaming broth
into paper bowls.

Placing them
in grateful hands.

FUTURE

Of course,
my parents
were shocked
by everything.

They blamed themselves.
Though they didn't
need to.

They wanted
to make sure
they had
a more hands-on role
in my future.

So they helped me
with applications
to community college.
We figured I could
get into one
even with my record.
While there,
I'd keep working on
my portfolio.
And the teachers at the Lodge
were happy to help.

Once I was
done with
community college,
hopefully I'd get into

a solid art program.
If that still
made sense
for me.

Emma came back
from overseas
at the end of summer.

She brought me
a book called
Secret Societies in Europe.

I don't know
how true or false
the book was.
But I wasn't
into reading
about those things
anymore.

It was good
to see
my sister again
in person.
She already
seemed older.

Seeing her
over a screen
just wasn't
the same.

LOOP

I think
that pretty much
catches us up.

I wanted
to end things
on a nice note.
A *happily ever after*.
Lesson learned
and all's well.

But nothing is ever
that simple.

Everything keeps
circling
back around.

The stairs go up
and
come back down.

The ring of fire
spins
on and on.

When I went into work
this morning,
the Lodge had
been attacked.

Windows shattered.
A gargoyle
smashed.
Graffiti
splattered
both inside and out.

The vandals
made it into
the building.
Kicked in doors.
Probably looking
for the
rumored tunnels.

Whoever did this
was a big fan
of the Cosmic Cat.

By the day's end
I found the animal
on three different walls.

I couldn't escape
its smile.
It wouldn't let me go
that easily.

Every line
of graffiti
cut at my nerves.

When I read
NEW WORLD ORDER SCUM,
it was talking
about me.

I worked at
the Lodge now.
So I was one of
the monsters.

And I couldn't
be angry
with the writer.

This was my fault
after all.

The flyers I printed
over the summer
were discovered
on the grounds.

I'd inspired
the vandals.

They'd found
the flyers.

They did
this
because
of
me.

I was
the source.

I was
the spark.

So here
I stand,
in the world
of my creation.

More real
than real.

I trace
the swirling letters.

Truth bombs
I might as well
have
dropped
myself.

Falling
all
around
me.

Bright
  spirals
    screaming.

WANT TO KEEP READING?

If you liked this book, check out another book from West 44 Books:

CONTROL ROOM
BY RYAN WOLF

ISBN: 9781538385203

HELIORAS WELCOMES YOU!

An Introduction
to the Present Moment

GROWTH

When he switches on
the lights,
my eyelids
snap
down.
Block out
the sudden white.

I hold myself
inside
the bright red
behind my lids.
Then blink
the room
into focus.

“How are you feeling,
Maggie?”
Terrance asks
with too much
sweetness.
“Are you well?
I feel
just terrible
about bringing you here
last night.

This was only
a misunderstanding.”

I won't say
anything.
I'm a child
tossed
in time-out.

I won't give
adult answers
to a man who isn't
my father.

Terrance leans in
to touch
my forehead.
His blond bangs
hang
over me.

"Your energy is low,"
he says
with his usual calm.
"But I don't judge you.
Or think
any less of you.

You don't think
less of a seed
because it isn't
a tree.

I know
the love inside you
will grow."

I won't say
anything.
Terrance tells us
life is only
where you place
your attention.

I want to
    throw it
        far away
            from here.

Into a melting memory.
A family vacation
when Dad was alive.
A morning bike ride
on a summer road.

Then maybe
    I won't be
    one more mind
    for Terrance's collection.

I try to
pull
up
memories
from my brain
    like weeds
    in the community garden.

Terrance's voice
    breaks through
    my thoughts.

"The pain
and punishment
of staying
in the Growth Room
is really a gift,"
          he says.
"Pain *is* growth,
in the body
and in the spirit.
And pain
is only
one stage.

          It's not
          the end.

It's not even
something
that lasts
          for very long.

We will get
to a better *now*
together.
Believe this."

I won't nod
and forgive.

          I won't say
          anything.
          Won't say
          anything.
          Won't say –

His hands
cup
my cheeks.

Terrance peers
into me.

His eyes
are like
windows
facing the sea.

He speaks
even more slowly,
even more gently.

"I know you
love your mum.
You sent that note
to the news
to protect her.

But you must
move beyond
your fear
for her safety.

No one is safe
in the end,"
he says.

I won't say
anything.

"I'm only here
to guide you,"
          he goes on.
"Further than
          your fears.

You can trust
the Helioras system.

It has worked.
And will continue
          to work.

          For your mum
          and for you."

My attention
          throws itself
                    to thoughts
                    of my mother.

Every piece of
hippie jewelry
she ever wore.
Promising
cosmic energies.
Bringing her
closer
to a
higher
state.

          Are we close now?
          Are we close?

I should've been
the mother
to my mother.

I should've never
let her
be charmed
by men
who promise
more than forever.

I can't let him
keep me
locked
away
from her.

In her gray jumpsuit.

Tearing
out
her
hair.

Hair going gray.

Mind going gray.

I can't hold
the words
in my chest
any longer.

"I'm grateful
for your mercy, Terrance,"
          I lie
          to those
          seaside windows.
"I'll never
do it again."

"Never do what,
my spark of sunlight?"
          he asks
          with a kind grin.

"I promise
not to contact
any outside media,"
          I tell him.
"I won't send
          any emails or calls
          to anyone."

"That's beautiful,"
          he says
          with a smile.
"What you did
was hurtful, though.
Directing evil
toward
the people
who love you.

          What would
          you say
          to them
          now?"

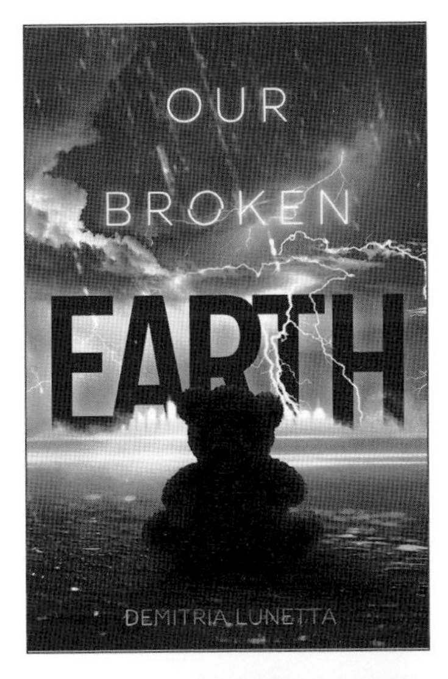
OUR
BROKEN
EARTH
DEMITRIA LUNETTA

THE
BEST
PART IS
AT THE
END

three
shots
KATY GRANT

THE
DRAGONS
CLUB

ABOUT THE AUTHOR

Ryan Wolf is the author of the young adult novels *Watches and Warnings* (2019) and *Control Room* (2020), as well as the *Creepy Critter Keepers* chapter book series for children. He has published stories, poems, essays, reviews, and journalism. Ryan holds his B.A. from Canisius College and his M.A. in the humanities from the University of Chicago. He currently resides in Buffalo, NY, with his wife and daughter.